We All Fall for Apples

*To Erika, Mara, and Scott—
the apples of my eye.
—E.S.H.*

*For my sister, Mrs. Berglund,
and her kindergarten class.
—A.V.K.*

Text copyright © 2002 by Emmi S. Herman.
Illustrations copyright © 2002 by Anne Kennedy.

All rights reserved. Published by Scholastic Inc.
SCHOLASTIC, CARTWHEEL BOOKS, and associated logos
are trademarks and/or registered trademarks of Scholastic Inc.
Lexile is a registered trademark of MetaMetrics, Inc.

Library of Congress Cataloging-in-Publication Data is available.

ISBN-13: 978-0-439-83312-7
ISBN-10: 0-439-83312-4

10 9 8 7 6   14/0

Printed in the U.S.A. 40 • This edition first printing, July 2008

We All Fall for Apples

LEVEL 1 · BEGINNING READER · 50-250 WORDS

By Emmi S. Herman

Illustrated by Anne Kennedy

Cartwheel BOOKS®

SCHOLASTIC INC.

New York Toronto London Auckland Sydney
Mexico City New Delhi Hong Kong Buenos Aires

Chapter 1

We are going to the farm.
We are going to pick apples.

Wait for Ruff!
Ruff wants to go, too.

We are going to the farm.
We are going to drink cider.

Wait for Sam!
Sam wants to go, too.

We are going to the farm.
We are going on a hayride.

Wait for Jan!
Jan wants to go, too.

We are going to the farm.

We are going to wait
for a new tire!

Chapter 2

We can fill a basket.
We can fill it with apples.

Oh, no! Too many apples.

We can fill a cup.
We can fill it with cider.

Oh, no! Too much cider.

We can fill a bag.
We can fill it with hay.

Oh, no! Too much hay.

We can fill a wagon.
We can fill it with people.

Oh, no! Too much fun!

We can fill a car.
We can fill it with sleepy people.

Too tired!

Chapter 3

Sam is making apple jam.

Mix and mash.
Add a dash.

Let it stand.

Jan is making apple bread.

Mix and mash.
Add a dash.

Let it bake.

Let it rise.

Apple jam and bread surprise!